SEA KEEPERS

The Rainbow
Seahorse

Coral Ripley

Special thanks to Sarah Hawkins
For Sullivan Rivers (Sulley)

ORCHARD BOOKS

First published in Great Britain in 2021 by The Watts Publishing Group

1 3 5 7 9 10 8 6 4 2

Text copyright © Orchard Books, 2021
Illustrations copyright © Orchard Books, 2021

A CIP catalogue record for this book
is available from the British Library.

ISBN 978 1 40836 366 9

Printed and bound in Great Britain by Clays Ltd, Elcograf S.p.A.

The paper and board used in this book are made from wood from responsible sources.

Orchard Books
An imprint of
Hachette Children's Group
Part of The Watts Publishing Group Limited
Carmelite House
50 Victoria Embankment
London EC4Y 0DZ

An Hachette UK Company
www.hachette.co.uk
www.hachettechildrens.co.uk

Contents

Chapter One

Emily was sitting on her bed, surrounded by a mountain of clothes.

"Whoa!" Mum said as she came in, wiping her hands on her apron. "Has there been a hurricane in here?"

Emily giggled. "I'm trying to decide what to wear for our fancy-dress party tonight!"

Mum grinned. "I can't believe it's

been a whole year since we opened the Mermaid Café."

Emily looked out of her window. Over the tops of the houses she could see the deep blue of the sea, twinkling in the morning sunshine, and seagulls swooping through the cloudless sky. She could hear the happy hum of people talking and chatting in the café downstairs, along with the chink of cups and the hiss of the coffee machine. She'd been so worried when they had first moved to Sandcombe, and now she never wanted to live anywhere else!

"I'm sure Grace and Layla can help you think of a costume," Mum told her.

"Maybe you should buy something new. I know – why don't you message them and I'll take you all shopping?"

Mum gave Emily her mobile and she quickly messaged her friends.

"Amanda, a timer's going off down here!" Dad shouted up the stairs.

"Ooh, my cake!" Mum jumped up. "Wait until you see it – it's going to be an amazing showstopper for the party!" Emily left the piles of clothes and followed her mother downstairs. She was excited to celebrate the café's first birthday, but she felt a bit nervous about the party, too. Unlike her friend Layla, she hated being the centre of attention. Maybe she could get a costume that helped her blend into the background, the way some animals could change colour to camouflage themselves.

Emily went down into the busy café

and breathed in the scent of delicious baking. "Mmmm, smells good, Mum!" she said.

Mum raced into the kitchen, while Emily grabbed her apron and started to help Dad, who threw her a grateful look.

"Excuse me, where are your plastic spoons? I want to stir my drink?" a lady asked Emily.

"Oh, we use these!" Emily said, offering her a tall glass jar with sticks of raw spaghetti in it.

"Spaghetti?" The lady scratched her head in confusion.

Emily nodded. "Pasta is better for the planet than plastic. If you use a plastic

spoon for a few seconds and then throw
it away, it stays in a rubbish heap for
thousands of years. Pasta doesn't."

"What a good idea!" the lady said approvingly. She helped herself to a piece of spaghetti and stirred her frothy coffee with it.

Emily was really proud that the Mermaid Café was plastic-free. She loved animals, and knew how plastic endangered them.

As she helped out with the customers, Emily reminded everyone about the fancy-dress party that evening. She was just gathering up some empty plates when she heard a familiar voice coming from behind her.

"Hellloooo!" Layla said dramatically. "I have a deadly disease and the only

cure for it is a cupcake."

Emily turned to see Layla and Grace standing by the glass display case, looking at the cupcakes inside it hungrily.

"Go on, then!" Dad said, handing Emily and her friends each a cupcake

with swirls of rainbow-coloured icing. Mermaid cupcakes were the café's speciality.

"You can eat them in the car," Mum said, pulling off her apron as she came out of the kitchen. "We've got shopping to do!"

Mum drove them to the nearest large town. The girls all sat in the back seat, munching their cupcakes. Looking out of the window at the big buildings and crowded streets they passed, Emily couldn't believe she used to live in an even bigger city than this. It all seemed too busy and loud now, compared to the peace and quiet of Sandcombe.

"Let's get a joint costume," Grace suggested when they got to the fancy-dress shop.

"What, like one with lots of arms and legs?" Layla looked confused. "Like an octopus?"

"No!" Grace laughed. "Three costumes that go together!"

"Good idea," said Emily, nodding. She knew she'd feel much better if she was in costume with her friends.

"Let's be a pop band!" Layla said, holding up a jazzy pink dress. "We can wear lots of make-up and dye our hair!"

"Hmmm, maybe no hair dye," Mum said. "Use coloured chalk instead."

"What about going as a sports team?" Grace suggested, holding up some plastic medals. She had plenty of real medals at home, from swimming competitions.

"Or we could all be animals?" Emily said as she found a bear costume. "The three bears, maybe?"

"Girls!" Mum called excitedly as she held something up. "I've got it!" She held up a glittery sequinned mermaid tail. "It's perfect for a party at the Mermaid Café!"

Emily glanced at her friends. Grace and Layla grinned back, and she knew they were all thinking the same thing. They didn't need to pretend to be mermaids, because they really were!

A year ago, when Emily had first moved to the seaside, she, Grace and Layla had rescued a dolphin together and met a mermaid princess. Princess Marina had been so grateful for their help, she'd taken them to the underwater city of Atlantis. There, Emily, Grace and Layla had been magically chosen to be Sea Keepers, whose job it was to help the mermaids by finding the hidden Golden Pearls. They had to find them before the evil siren Effluvia did, otherwise she would use their powerful magic to free her siren sisters and take over the mermaid kingdom!

Emily glanced down at the purple shell

bracelet around her wrist. Grace and
Layla both had one exactly the same.
Mum thought they were just friendship
bracelets, but they were so much more
than that. Every time the mermaids
needed the Sea Keepers' help, the
bracelets glowed with magic!

"Well, what do you think?" Mum asked, still holding up the costume.

Emily looked at the mermaid tail. It was nowhere near as beautiful as her  real one. Emily took the tail from Mum reluctantly. It was made out of scratchy material with hundreds of plastic sequins sewn on it.

Mum was still waiting for her to say something.

"It's pretty," Emily said hesitantly.

Since she had started being a Sea Keeper Emily had learnt so much about how human rubbish was affecting the seas. Even tiny things like sequins were a huge problem – if a sequin got washed into the ocean it could be eaten by a fish. A real mermaid would hate all the plastic on this fake tail.

"I don't know, Mum . . ." Emily started, but before she could finish Grace interrupted.

"Let's go and try them on," Grace said, hustling Emily and Layla into the changing room.

"I don't think—" Emily started, but Grace cut her off.

"Look!" She grinned and held up her wrist. Purple light filled the changing room. Their shell bracelets were glowing. The mermaids needed them!

Chapter Two

Emily, Layla and Grace squished together in the tiny changing room and whispered the magic words that Marina had taught them:

"Take me to the ocean blue,
Sea Keepers to the rescue!"

Magic swirled around them, making the changing-room curtain flutter. No time would pass while they were away,

so Emily's mum would never even know that they'd been off on a secret mermaid adventure!

Emily closed her eyes as the magic whirled around, and when she opened them again she was underwater. Her legs had been replaced by a beautiful golden mermaid tail!

"Wahhhoooo!" Layla shrieked, splashing her pink tail fins.

"Welcome back, Sea Keepers," a familiar voice said from behind them. Emily turned to see a mermaid, slightly older than she was, with a lilac tail and pinky-purple hair. As well as the shell crown she always wore, Marina was also

24

wearing a delicate pearl-and-silver mask.
But it didn't cover up her smile – or the
happiness in her eyes.

"Princess Marina!"
Emily swam over
to hug her
mermaid friend.

Marina
squeezed her
tightly. "I'm
so pleased to
see you!" she
said happily.

"Us too!"
Layla looked around
curiously. "Where are we this time?"

"And why are you wearing a mask?"
Grace added.

Emily glanced around at their
surroundings. The water was clear
and deep blue, and the sandy seabed
was covered with tufts of grass, like an
underwater field. But that wasn't the
most amazing thing. Behind Marina,
two tall stone pillars towered up from the
seabed.

"I saw columns like this when I went on
holiday to Italy!" Layla said.

Emily swam over to touch the smooth
stone. The pillars looked like something
from the human world – so what were
they doing underwater?

"Come with me!" Marina said. She swam through a gap in the columns, and the girls followed. As she swam between the pillars, Emily felt tiny bubbles bursting around her and knew what that meant – mermaid magic!

They swam into an underwater city full of marble buildings and white statues. All around them floated hundreds of seahorses, shimmering like tiny, colourful jewels. Emily turned to look at some near her and the seahorses scattered as she moved. They reminded her of butterflies fluttering about!

"Welcome to the Hidden City!" Marina announced.

"It looks like an ancient human city," Grace said.

Marina nodded. "It used to be above the water, but it flooded thousands of years ago. No one remembers it's here, and mermaid magic keeps it hidden. The seahorses have made this their home. They are very shy creatures, but once a year the mermaids are invited to come here for the Seahorse Ball."

"The Seahorse Ball!" Layla repeated, her eyes wide with wonder. "Is that a party – with seahorses?" She clapped her hands excitedly.

For once, Marina looked almost as excited as Layla. "Yes! It's one of

the most magical nights in the aqua
calendar," she said, grinning. "Mermaids
come from all around the world to see
the seahorses dance, and they announce
the King and Queen of the Ball –
the seahorse couple that are the best
dancers."

Emily's eyes widened in anticipation.
She wasn't keen on parties, but dancing
seahorses sounded amazing!

"Ooh, and it must be a masked ball!"
Layla guessed, looking at the pretty mask
over Marina's eyes.

Marina nodded as she took it off to
show it to the girls. "This mask has been
in the royal family for generations, and

it's only worn at the Seahorse Ball.
It belonged to my ancestor, Queen
Nerissa."

"The one who hid the Golden Pearls?"
asked Emily, remembering the story
Marina had once told them.

"Yes," said Marina. "She defeated the
sirens and banished them from Atlantis.
Then she scattered the pearls across the
seas to keep them safe."

"Does the Mystic Clam think there's
a pearl here?" Grace asked. The Mystic
Clam was so old he knew where Queen
Nerissa had hidden the pearls.

Marina nodded seriously now. "He
gave me this riddle," she said.

"In the city that opens once a year,
The pearl sits like a falling tear.
Under an eye that cannot glance,
Except to see true love's dance."

"'*The city that opens once a year*' – that has to be the Hidden City," Marina told them, waving her hand around. A purple and gold seahorse flitted out of her way.

"Sorry," she said, giggling. Then she gave a deep sigh. "I wish you were just here for the party! The mermaid world is so wonderful when Effluvia isn't trying to spoil it."

"That's why we have to find the pearls and keep it that way!" Grace said, her

eyes shining with determination.

"Besides – we can party and fight Effluvia at the same time," Layla said.

"It's great to just be here," Emily said, looking at the clouds of tiny seahorses. They were getting braver and swimming closer, staring at the new arrivals curiously. About as long as Emily's finger, the seahorses had curling tails and delicate snouts. The little fins on their back fluttered like a horse's mane as they swam. They were so amazing!

As Emily watched, the seahorses gathered in a circle around an ornate fountain. Emily swam closer so that she could see what they were all looking

33

at. In the middle of the fountain, two seahorses began to dance.

"Oh, it's Lena and Luca!" Marina called out, beckoning the girls over.

Emily stared at the seahorses in delight as they twirled together, their tails entwined. One was purple and one was gold, but as she watched they changed colours, from silver to bright green to a light sky blue.

They spiralled up though the water, their tiny fins rippling like a hummingbird's wings as they twisted and turned, then finally they came together and touched noses, turning a deep shade of red. The watching seahorses cheered

and fluttered their
fins in appreciation.
The Sea Keepers
joined in, clapping
as loudly as they
could.

"Who are Lena
and Luca?" Grace
asked Marina.

"They were
crowned King
and Queen of the
Seahorse Ball last
year, and the year
before that too,"
Marina told them.

"It would take a really special couple to beat them this year."

Emily glanced over at Lena and Luca, who were bowing to the crowd. Then Luca twirled Lena around, making the watching seahorses cheer even louder. "*'Except to see true love's dance'*!" she gasped, remembering the Mystic Clam's riddle. "That must mean Lena and Luca!"

"Maybe they can help us find the pearl?" Grace suggested.

"And show me some dance moves." Layla tried to copy one of their twists. "They're really good!"

But before they could talk to them,

Lena and Luca swam away and the other seahorses dispersed.

"They have to get ready for the ball," a small yellow seahorse told them.

"You must be excited," Layla said.

The yellow seahorse nodded. "I just wish I could dance like them. They're definitely going to be crowned King and Queen again this year."

"Well, you don't have to win to have fun!" Layla told him.

"I'm sure you're a good dancer too!" Emily said kindly, reaching out to him. The seahorse curled his tail around her finger and turned bright pink with embarrassment.

"I can never remember the moves for the seahorse shimmy. I think it's left fin, right fin, tail, tail, tail," he said. "Or is it right fin, left fin, tail, tail, tail?" Letting go of Emily's finger, the seahorse tried it both ways. He wasn't as graceful as Lena and Luca, and as he concentrated he turned blotchy purple. Panting, he swam back over to the Sea Keepers. "And I can't get the colour changes right, either. Whenever I see Iris I go pink, I just can't help it!"

"Who's Iris?" Grace asked.

"Only the most beautiful seahorse in the whole wide ocean!" he said with a dreamy sigh. "She's my girlfriend. And

she's a really good dancer. She could definitely be queen of the ball, but I'm not good enough to be the king. I wish I could remember the moves so that I don't let her down."

Emily glanced at the others, and knew they were thinking the same thing she was. They needed to solve the riddle and find the pearl, but as part of their Sea Keeper promise they'd pledged to help all sea creatures – and this little seahorse definitely needed their help!

Chapter Three

Emily looked at the sad little seahorse bobbing in the water. "We can help you learn the seahorse shimmy!" she said gently. "Layla's a really good dancer."

"Really?" The seahorse's eyes went wide. "You'd do that for me? Thank you so much, Sea Keepers!"

"What's your name?" Grace asked.

"I'm Hari," the little seahorse said,

going back to his original yellow colour.

"Come on then, Hari, let's help you impress Iris!" Emily told him.

"Show me the moves again. I'll try and help," Layla said.

Layla watched as Hari swam forward. He put his snout down and flapped the two fins at the side of his head that looked a bit like sticky-out ears. He pushed out his tummy and twisted from one side to another.

Emily didn't know much about seahorse dancing – but she could see the difference between this routine and the one they'd seen earlier. Lena and Luca had been so graceful, and Hari just . . . wasn't.

"At the end everyone finishes with a big move," Hari said. "I thought I could do this?" His tail turned purple and his head went bright red. His middle was sort of blotchy brown. "What do you think?" Hari said.

"Um, very colourful," Emily said kindly.

"Did I look like a rainbow?" Hari asked.

"Oh, was that what it was!" Grace exclaimed. "Sorry," she added quickly when she saw his disappointed face.

"How about we think of a big dance move to go with the rainbow?" Layla suggested tactfully.

Emily grinned as Layla took charge.

Her friend was great at
performing. If anyone
could help Hari, Layla
could.

"How about if you do
a pirouette?" Layla said.
"I'll show you how." She
pointed her fins and did
a quick spin through
the water, holding her
hands over her head like
a ballerina.

"Beautiful!" Marina
cheered.

Hari straightened his
tail and spun around as

fast as he could. "It's making me dizzy!" he said, wobbling through the water. Grace held out her finger and he clung to it gratefully.

"Pick one spot and stare at it. That will stop you from getting dizzy," Layla told him. The next time Hari tried it was much better.

"That was great!" Layla said, and he glowed gold with pride.

Layla, Emily and Grace practised the seahorse shimmy with Hari until he could do it with his eyes shut.

"Luca and Lena had better watch out!" Marina joked.

"Seriously, that was great," Grace said.

"Iris is going to love it," Layla teased.

"Thank you so much for helping me," Hari said. "Is there anything I can do for you?"

"We need to get to the ball," Marina said. "Where is it being held this year?"

"At the Grand Plaza. Follow me!" Hari said, swimming away. The girls and Marina followed him, but although Hari's fins were whirring, he wasn't moving very fast.

"Can I give you a lift?" Emily suggested, holding out her finger.

Hari curled his tail around her little finger and Emily cupped her other hand around him gently. Marina and the

Sea Keepers kicked their fins and sped through the water, following the tiny seahorse's directions through the ancient underwater city.

"It's kind of spooky, thinking about the people that must have lived here long ago," Layla said.

"I think it's really interesting," Grace added.

"And beautiful!" Emily said. The walls and buildings were still standing exactly as they must have been before the city sank. And all around the city were incredible statues. They had to be thousands of years old, but they still looked brand new!

"The mermaid magic that keeps the city hidden protects it too," Marina explained. "Without the magic, it would all crumble very quickly."

Emily gasped as they passed a marble statue of a girl holding a jug. She looked so real, even though there were colourful sea anemones growing around her legs and seahorses flitting around her long, carved hair.

Hari nudged Emily with his snout. "Wait until you see the beautiful statues in the Grand Plaza," he told her. "They're the six guardians of the city and they each represent a different emotion. There it is, up ahead."

Hari pointed at a huge square surrounded by marble walls.

As they got closer, Marina gave an excited squeal. "I can't wait to find out what my costume is! Every year there's a different theme for the ball and the doors are enchanted so that when you swim through them your costume magically appears!" She clapped her hands in excitement. "Last year's theme was coral and my costume was a bright coral-pink dress that trailed down to my fins. It was so pretty!"

"I liked the twinkle year," Hari said.

"Oh yes!" Marina said. "That year the ball was held at midnight. The ballroom

was dark, but all our costumes were decorated with bioluminescent algae that shone like stars in the sky. It was so beautiful." She sighed happily as she remembered.

"I wonder what this year's theme will be," Layla said. "I hope we get to wear something really amazing!"

Even Emily felt excited to find out what the theme would be. Maybe it would give them an idea for what to wear to the fancy-dress party back at home!

The girls approached the entrance.

A mermaid with a dark purple tail and a midnight-blue mask greeted them with a friendly smile. "Hello, I'm Effie. Come

50

in, come in!" she said, beckoning them to come inside.

Marina put her royal mask on and

swam through the doors. The Sea Keepers exchanged excited glances, and then Emily followed her in. She couldn't wait to see what her magical costume would look like!

Chapter Four

Inside the plaza, the water was dim and murky green. Emily looked down to see what costume she'd been given, expecting a beautiful dress.

"Oh . . ." she said sadly. Instead of a gown, she was wearing a shapeless dirty grey plastic tunic.

She peered through the dark water in confusion to see what Marina was

wearing. The mermaid princess looked puzzled by her dress, which seemed to be made of bin liners.

Grace swam over to Emily. "This wasn't what I was expecting," she murmured. She was wearing a mask covered with bottle caps and sweet wrappers instead of precious gems, but Emily could see the disappointment in her eyes. Emily touched her own face and realised that she was wearing a mask, too. From the way Grace was staring at her, she guessed that hers looked the same as her friend's.

Finally, Layla came swimming into the plaza with an excited squeal that faded

54

away as she looked down at her new outfit. Like the others, she was wearing a mask decorated with rubbish and an outfit made of plastic bags.

That wasn't all. The water was so dirty that they could barely see the six guardian statues dotted around the square. Mermaids and seahorses were gathered in the corners, chatting in low voices, but no one looked like they were having any fun.

"Let's go ask them what the theme is," Marina said, shaking her head as she tried to make sense of the strange scene in front of them.

One pink seahorse had its tail wrapped

around a cotton bud, the kind people use to clean their ears. Another was clinging on to a plastic straw. Emily knew that there was rubbish in the sea – but why was it here, at the ball?

As they swam through the water, things got worse and worse. The band was made up of hermit crabs, but they were using old rubbish for shells. One was inside a margarine tub, another had a yoghurt pot and the last had a rusty cola can. Instead of decorations there were strange ghostly things floating in the murky water. For a second Emily thought they were jellyfish, until she realized they were plastic bags.

Hari tugged on her finger, pointing his snout at the nearest statue. "This one shows happiness," he said. It was a tall lady with two long plaits, holding a baby. There was a warm smile on the statue's face – but nobody else in the plaza looked very happy.

"Something is badly wrong," Marina said, frowning.

They swam over to a group of mermaids, who were huddled together in one corner.

"I just can't imagine what the theme is," one was saying in a low voice.

"Maybe it's some kind of joke?" another muttered, looking at her plastic-bag

costume. More and more mermaids arrived until the Grand Plaza was filled. But none of the guests seemed in the mood to dance.

"Call this a party? Nobody's dancing," boomed a voice from across the room. "There isn't even any music."

Emily turned to see Effie, the mermaid who had welcomed them at the door. The mermaid removed her mask and shook out her long, midnight-blue hair.

Emily groaned. Effie was really Effluvia!

"Well, if you want me to sing, I can!" Effluvia continued. The siren pulled herself up to her full height and her purple tail swished like an angry cat's.

Then she opened her mouth and let out a high note. The sound echoed around the square. The Sea Keepers instinctively put their hands over their ears, but Effluvia's siren song wasn't directed at them. Eventually the magical music died away and was replaced by a wicked laugh.

Effluvia swam to the middle of the square, followed by an ugly fish with long pointed teeth and a light hanging from his forehead.

"Who's that guy?" Hari whispered as he floated by Emily's ear.

"That's Fang, Effluvia's pet anglerfish," Emily explained. Her mind was racing. What had Effluvia done with that magic song? She knew the siren well enough to know it wouldn't be anything good.

"Welcome, everyone, to this year's Seahorse Ball." Effluvia spread her hands out graciously as she spoke. "I hope you like my pollution theme. I thought since we were inviting humans to join us,"

she glared at Emily, Grace and Layla, "that we should use all the little gifts the two-legs leave us. I now declare the ball – and the Hidden City – open!" Effluvia crowed. "Although we might have to rename it the Un-Hidden City. Now that I've broken the mermaid magic protecting it, this won't be 'the city that opens once a year' any more! Everyone will be able to see it. Although they'll have to be quick – without the magic, it won't last for long!" Effluvia threw back her head and let out another cackle.

Grace shuddered.

"She's so horrible," Layla said.

"Don't worry," Emily reassured Hari,

whose fins were quivering with fear. "We won't let her ruin your home."

But Grace shook her head. "It's not just that. She said *'the city that opens once a year'*. She knows the riddle!"

Effluvia grinned nastily. "Yes, I know your precious riddle! This time I'm way ahead of you, two-legs. I'm going to get that pearl, and there's nothing you can do about it!"

Chapter Five

As the mermaid magic that had
protected the underwater city vanished,
the plaza's statues and walls instantly
started showing their age, turning green.
Cracks began to appear in the marble,
and the statues started to crumble.

The brightly coloured seahorses
scattered as bits of stone fell off the
statues. Emily cupped Hari in her hands

and Marina jumped into action.

"Quick, we have to help," she told the other mermaids. "Everyone, use your magic to protect the city." She began to sing a beautiful song that echoed round the plaza, and all the other mermaids joined in:

"Sing to save the city,
Where people used to roam.
Mermaid magic true and strong,
Save the seahorses' home."

As the song died away, a protective bubble appeared around the Grand Plaza. The water was still murky, with bits of rubbish floating around, but thanks to the mermaid magic, the statues and

pillars weren't crumbling quite as fast.

"We won't be able to hold it for long,"
Marina said, turning to Grace, Emily and
Layla with a worried look on her face.
"The only way to save the city is to find
the Golden Pearl and use its power."

"But how did Effluvia know the riddle?" Layla wondered.

"I don't know, but we've got to solve it before she does," Grace said, putting her hands on her hips.

"What is it again?" Emily asked her.

Marina repeated the Mystic Clam's words:

"In the city that opens once a year,
The pearl sits like a falling tear.
Under an eye that cannot glance,
Except to see true love's dance."

"'*True love's dance*' is obviously Lena and Luca," Layla said.

"But what's '*an eye that cannot glance*'?" Grace wondered out loud. Next

to them a small chunk of the happiness
statue broke off and fell through the
water.

"A statue!" Marina realised, clicking
her fingers. "They have eyes, but they
can't see."

"*'The pearl sits like a falling tear',*"
Emily murmured thoughtfully. "Is there a
statue for sadness?" she asked.

The girls looked round at all the
guardian statues.

"That one is for bravery," said Marina,
pointing to a muscled man holding up
a sword. As they watched, the tip of the
sword broke off and fell on to the seabed,
making the sand billow.

"Let's split up and look," Grace suggested. She raced across the plaza to the statue furthest away, a man looking terrified with his mouth forming an 'O' of surprise.

"Wait for me!" Hari called. Emily held out her finger and the little seahorse wrapped his tail around it again. Emily stroked his nose gently. "It'll be OK," she said, sounding more certain than she felt. "We've stopped Effluvia before." *Although this time she knows the riddle. What if she gets to the pearl first?* she thought anxiously.

"This one looks like Effluvia!" Layla called, pointing at the statue

representing
anger. It was a
lady with her
face twisted
in fury. Layla
swam over to
it and pulled a
comically cross
face that made
Emily laugh.
Even when
she was feeling
worried, Emily's friends could always
make her smile.

Holding Hari gently, she swam through
the murky water, batting plastic bags out

of the way until she got to a statue of a man, holding his tummy as he laughed at a joke told centuries ago.

Then Grace called from across the plaza. "Got it! Over here!" Emily kicked her fins and sped over to her, with Layla and Marina right behind her.

Grace was floating in front of a statue of an old man, his face twisted in grief. Under his stone eyes, a single tear was carved.

As Emily peered through the misty water, she spotted a glow of gold. It had to be the pearl!

But as she swam closer, she saw another golden glow, then another, until there

were four yellow dots. *Four pearls?* Emily
thought in confusion. Then two tiny
seahorses swam out from behind the
statue – Lena and Luca.

The glow wasn't coming from the statue, it was coming from the strange yellow light in their eyes. The seahorses were under Effluvia's spell!

Chapter Six

Hari gasped, and Emily looked down
to see the little seahorse turning white
with fear. She stroked his bumpy back as
reassuringly as she could.

Lena and Luca were both a deep
bruised purple, the same colour as
Effluvia's tail, as they swam out of the
statue's shadow in perfect unison.

"Good work, my seahorse spies."

Effluvia gave a mocking laugh as she saw the Sea Keepers' horrified faces. "Yes, Lena and Luca overheard your riddle earlier and told it to me. Genius that I am, I've cracked it already. All I have to do is get them to dance in front of the statue, and the pearl will be mine!" She clapped her hands in delight. "Then I will release my siren sisters, we will rule the underwater world and you mermaids will be forced to bow to us." She glared at the mermaids who were still working to protect the Hidden City.

Emily grabbed Marina and Layla's hands.

"We'll never bow to you," Grace said,

looking braver than the statue with the sword.

"I am telling you that this time I *will* get that pearl," Effluvia said, her voice cold with fury. "And I'm not letting you pathetic two-legs stop me." She raised her arms up high and took a deep breath. The girls instantly covered their ears as Effluvia started to sing a magical song:

"Stony statues under the sea,
Hear my song and obey ME!"

As her voice echoed through the murky water, there was a loud thump, and then another.

"What's happening?" Emily whispered.

"Look!" Layla said as she pointed.

The happiness statue was walking though the water towards them, her eyes filled with the same yellow glow as Lena and Luca's! The bravery statue staggered towards them, too, brandishing his broken sword. The statues were coming to life – and they were following Effluvia's orders!

The siren sang a low note, and stone arms closed around Emily's chest. She struggled and thrashed her tail, but the bravery statue picked her up and held her fast.

"Stop! Stop!" cried Hari. But there was nothing he could do. He was much too little to fight off the statue.

The anger statue grabbed Grace, who fought back. She churned up the water as she thrashed against the statue. But it was no good; the statue was too strong. She wrapped a stone arm around Grace's tail, gripping her tight. Marina was pinned by the fear statue, and Layla was

held by the laughing man. His stone face was still grinning, but Layla didn't look happy at all as she struggled to break free from her stone captor. Only the crying statue stayed where he was.

"Don't be sad, Sea Keepers," sneered Effluvia. "You've got front row seats to watch the show!" She let out a trilling laugh then commanded, "Seahorses, DANCE!"

Lena and Luca floated in front of the sadness statue and began to twirl. The dance was every bit as beautiful as it had been before, but Emily could hardly bear to watch it this time. Effluvia had won. She was going to get the pearl.

The seahorses twisted and twirled together gracefully. As before, they both turned red for the finale.

Effluvia turned to the sadness statue, a triumphant look on her face. But nothing happened.

"Where is my pearl?" Effluvia shouted, going up to the statue and knocking on its head with her fist. "Dance again!" she snarled at the seahorses. "Do it properly this time! Do the dance of TRUE LOVE. Now!"

The yellow light in Lena and Luca's eyes glowed under Effluvia's spell and they started their dance again.

Emily glanced at Grace and Layla. She

felt a tiny bit of hope. Maybe they hadn't solved the riddle yet? There was still a chance they could stop Effluvia from getting the pearl!

All around them, mermaids and seahorses were peeking out from the gloom and watching the dance. As it finished again, there was still no pearl. Effluvia let out a screech of fury. She grabbed the nearest seahorse, and next to her Emily heard Hari gasp.

"No!" he cried out. "That's Iris! Effluvia's got my girlfriend!"

"Why isn't it working?" Effluvia yelled, holding the little blue seahorse up to her eyes. Iris tried to wriggle away, but

Effluvia was clutching her as tightly as
the statues were gripping the girls.

"I don't know!" Iris squeaked.

"Let her go!" Emily yelled bravely.

Effluvia turned to her, narrowing her

eyes in anger. "Be quiet," she said, "or I'll let Fang have this seahorse as a snack!" Her anglerfish swam out from behind her, his light illuminating the very hungry look on his face . . .

Chapter Seven

Emily, Marina, Grace and Layla struggled against the statues as Effluvia held the tiny seahorse tightly in her hand.

"Can I eat her now, Effluvia?" Fang whined. "I'm starving."

"Quiet! I'm trying to think," Effluvia snapped. Then she turned to the girls with a cruel grin. "I will get the truth,

even if I have to squeeze it out of you."
She opened her mouth and sang a long
note. As the tune rose higher and higher,
Emily felt the statue's arms get tighter,
squeezing the breath out of her, just like
Effluvia was squeezing Iris!

Suddenly Emily noticed a frantic
movement in front of her – Hari! The
seahorse had turned black with fury, and
his fins were whirring so fast that they
were a blur.

"Iris!" he called, swimming towards his
girlfriend as fast as he could.

He was so small Effluvia didn't even
notice him coming. But what could he do
against the powerful siren?

Hari hooked his tail in Effluvia's hair and pulled hard, yanking her head back. Effluvia was so shocked she stopped singing and let go of Iris, who swam out of her fist and over to Hari. Together, they tugged on the siren's hair. Effluvia batted at her head,

trying to swat the seahorses, but they ducked out of the way.

"Fang! Get them! Eat them ALL!"

Effluvia shrieked at her anglerfish.

"Quick!" Grace yelled. Emily saw her friend pushing herself out of the anger statue's grip. She looked up and saw the yellow light had faded from the bravery statue's eyes, and its arms had loosened too. Hari had interrupted Effluvia's song, breaking the spell! She pushed the statue's arms away and slipped out of the gap.

"I'm stuck!" Marina called. The girls gathered together and tugged her free of the fear statue's grasp.

"Where did they go?" Fang moaned. "I'm hungry!"

"Get back here!" Effluvia screeched as

she searched for the seahorses. "I'm going to get you, you deep-sea donkeys!"

Layla giggled and nudged Emily. Iris and Hari were hidden by the sadness statue, their bodies blending into the pale white and green algae. Their tails were tangled together and they touched snouts lovingly.

Effluvia was still crashing around, swimming and shouting, and Fang was snapping his jaws as he moaned about his lost dinner, but the two seahorses were so in love they didn't even flinch.

Suddenly Emily had an idea. Hari and Iris were really in love. True love wasn't flashy and impressive like Luca

and Lena's dance. She thought about
the sound of her parents laughing as
they cleaned up after a long day at the
café, or dancing along to a song on the
radio in the kitchen. True love was being
happy to be together, no matter what.

"I think the true love in the riddle
could be Hari and Iris," she whispered to
the others.

"It's worth a try!" said Grace.

As Effluvia continued to rant and rave,
the girls swam over to Hari and Iris.
"Dance for us please!" Emily said. "Right
in front of the statue!"

"Us?" Hari asked, looking surprised.
Iris blushed bright pink.

Emily nodded.

"But I won't be any good—" Hari started.

"You'll be brilliant," Layla told him. "Just have fun with Iris."

"Please hurry," Emily said, watching Effluvia. "There's no time to explain." The siren's temper tantrum wouldn't last for long, and then she'd notice what they were up to.

Hari and Iris took up position in front of the sadness statue. They bowed, then started to dance. They weren't as polished and graceful as Luca and Lena, but their dance was lovely in its own way. As Hari showed off his new rainbow

91

pirouette, Iris got the giggles. He spun her around too, and they both changed colours as they shimmied and twirled. Hari and Iris were having so much fun it didn't matter that their moves were a bit messy.

Emily peered at the statue, holding her breath expectantly as she waited for the golden pearl to appear. Surely this was true love's dance. So where was the Golden Pearl?

Emily felt like she was going to cry. She lifted up her mask and wiped her eyes. Next to her, Layla sighed.

"I was so sure that was it!" Marina said sadly. Emily turned to give her a

comforting hug – and gasped! There, glowing on Marina's royal mask, was the pearl! It glistened just under her eye like a tear.

"Look!" she gasped, pointing.

But Emily wasn't the only one who had seen it.

"The pearl!" Effluvia shrieked. She shoved the sadness statue, sending it crashing on to the seabed as she sped towards them.

"Seahorses, dance!" Grace yelled. "Do the seahorse shimmy!" All the seahorses swam on to the dance floor, filling the water with their colourful bodies.

Effluvia batted the seahorses out of the way as they whirled and twirled in front of her like colourful confetti, but it gave the Sea Keepers the time they needed.

Emily picked the pearl off Marina's mask, then the others grabbed her hands.

"I wish the Hidden City was protected again!" she cried.

Bubbles of mermaid magic fizzed around them and the golden light disappeared from the pearl. The murky water instantly turned clear and the statues returned to their normal places, looking clean and new. Best of all, the mermaids' plastic-bag costumes changed

to beautiful dresses and their masks were now covered with shimmering pink and white pearls.

"AAARRRGGGHHH!" Effluvia screeched in fury, grabbing Fang's fin just as he was about to catch a seahorse in his huge jaws.

"Nooo!" Fang wailed.

"Hurrah!" cheered the mermaids and seahorses. "Long live the Sea Keepers!"

Layla, Grace and Emily grinned at each other. They'd saved the city – and now they could enjoy the most amazing mermaid ball ever!

Chapter Eight

Marina took off the royal mask and stared at it in amazement. "I can't believe there was a Golden Pearl hidden on here the whole time!" she said. "My great-great-grandmother must have known we'd keep it safe."

Lena and Luca swam over shaking their heads. The weird yellow glow had gone from their eyes – they weren't under

Effluvia's spell any more.

"We're so sorry. We didn't want to help her, but had to do what she said," Lena said in a soft voice.

"It's OK, don't worry," Emily reassured her. She remembered with a shudder how helpless she'd felt when Effluvia had tried to cast a spell on the Sea Keepers, the first time they'd become mermaids. "You didn't have any choice."

"I knew it wouldn't work," Luca said. "Lena and I are best friends . . ."

" . . . And brilliant dance partners," Lena added, "but we're not in love."

They looked over at where Hari and Iris were floating, their tails still

98

entwined. There was no mistaking their love for each other.

Hari glanced at Iris, who nodded. "We wanted you to be the first to know," he told them, blushing. "We're going to get married!"

"Congratulations!" Marina said.

"Wow!" said Emily.

"I'm really happy for you!" Grace said.

"It's so romantic!" Layla said.

"UGH!" Effluvia spat. "All this love is more disgusting than two-legs' rubbish. You got lucky this time, Sea Keepers, but next time I will get that pearl, and then the whole sea will bow to ME!" She flung her hair over her shoulder and swam off, still holding Fang, who looked back at the seahorses hungrily.

As they left, there was a sound of trumpeting, and Emily jumped.

"Don't worry," Marina grinned, "it's just the trumpet fish." Two large fish,

with noses that did look surprisingly like trumpets, gave another tooting blast. "It's time for the ball to begin!"

This time, the Grand Plaza was filled with cheerful chatter, music and beautiful costumes – all dripping with pearls. One mermaid had a dress so long that it came down to the tips of her fins. She was dancing with a mermaid whose long, green hair was the exact same shade as her mint-coloured gown. A merman wearing a tuxedo jacket swam over to them and bowed.

"Isn't it amazing?" Layla breathed. She had on a flowing aquamarine dress that matched her tail perfectly.

Emily nodded. She looked down at her golden gown, studded with tiny pearls. It was the most beautiful thing she had ever worn.

"This is so cool!" said Grace, spinning around so that her long, pale-pink dress swished through the water.

The hermit-crab band, who now had pearl-encrusted shells, started up and a hush fell over the room. Then the seahorses swam into the middle and lined up. Hari and Iris were right next to Luca and Lena, looking nervous and happy.

The seahorse shimmy began, with all the seahorses moving perfectly in time to the music. Layla started doing the moves

too and Emily had to nudge her with her elbow to stop her friend from getting carried away!

"Uh oh!" Grace said. Hari had forgotten the moves and was completely out of time. But Iris just giggled and the two seahorses jigged around, doing their own thing, turning every colour of the rainbow as they danced.

The mermaids nearby started murmuring to each other as they watched. Emily hoped Hari wasn't going to get into trouble. But to her surprise, Luca and Lena nodded at each other – and started copying Hari and Iris! Everyone laughed, and Emily felt herself

relax. One by one, all the other seahorses stopped doing the formal moves and started to dance freestyle, moving to the music in the way that made them happy.

"I'm not missing this party!" Layla laughed, dragging the others on to

the dance floor. Soon everyone in the ballroom had joined in, mermaids and seahorses dancing to the music from the hermit-crab band.

The girls were breathless and happy when the music stopped and Marina swam to the front of the room. "The votes are in. It's time to crown the King and Queen of the ball!" She paused dramatically.

The dancers whispered among themselves excitedly as they waited for the princess to continue.

Marina grinned from ear to ear. "I am absolutely delighted to announce that the King and Queen of this year's ball

are . . . Hari and Iris!" she declared.

Hari and Iris both blushed pink, but the other seahorses cheered – Luca and Lena loudest of all.

Marina put tiny crowns on the winners'

heads as Hari and Iris twisted their tails together. Then King Hari and Queen Iris bowed to the band, who started playing a new song.

Layla, Grace and Emily danced around the plaza in a huge conga line led by a real conga eel. Worn out from dancing, Emily took her friends aside.

"This party might be nearly over, but there's another one we need to get ready for," she said.

"Two parties – this is the best day ever!" Layla said, grinning.

"Wasn't the ball fun?" Marina said. "I'm so glad you got to come."

"Me too," Emily said. "It was the best,

but I think it's time for us to go home now."

Marina nodded. "But you have to come back next year!"

"Deal!" Grace said, shaking Marina's hand.

They waved goodbye to their seahorse friends, then Marina sang the magic words that would take them home:

"Send the Sea Keepers back to land,
Until we need them to lend a hand".

Bubbles of mermaid magic swirled round them and a second later they were back in the changing room, holding the plastic mermaid tails. "Wow, that was an amazing adventure," Layla said.

"I'm so pleased Hari and Iris were chosen as King and Queen of the ball." Grace said, sighing happily. "It was the perfect ending."

Emily looked down at the mermaid costume and felt funny. After seeing all

the plastic and rubbish in the Hidden City, she felt bad about buying more.

"Do you think we could make our costumes?" she asked her friends. "Then we wouldn't have to buy more plastic."

"We could wear our swimming things and make tails," Grace said practically.

"Ooh, I've got an old dress we could recycle!" Layla said excitedly. "We could use the material to make tails, and stick things on them to look like scales. I've got loads of craft supplies at home."

They linked arms and walked out of the changing rooms.

"No good?" Mum asked.

"We're going to make our own

mermaid costumes out of recycled things instead," Emily told her.

"Great idea," Mum said, planting a kiss on the top of her head.

It took all afternoon, but finally Emily, Layla and Grace were ready to go to the party in their home-made mermaid costumes. Over her shiny turquoise swimming costume, Emily had pinned a skirt made out of Layla's dress, with two wide panels to be the fins. They flopped about a bit as she walked, but Emily didn't mind. They'd gone down to the beach to collect shells, and they'd stuck them on and painted scales with colourful fabric paint. Layla had put dots

all over hers to be like the pearls in their costumes for the ball. Emily felt so proud as they went into the café. Her costume wasn't going to hurt any sea creatures – and she'd had so much fun making it with her friends.

"You look amazing!" Mum exclaimed as they walked in. She was dressed like a flower fairy with a daisy crown and some old fairy wings, and she was just finishing icing a beautiful cake that looked exactly like the Mermaid Café. "Our little eco-mermaids." Mum grinned as she hugged them all.

"No, we're Sea Keepers!" Layla corrected her without thinking.

"Sea Keepers, I like that!" said Dad, who was dressed as a pirate. "Well, here's to the first year of the Mermaid Café, and to our three Sea Keepers!"

Emily, Grace and Layla grinned at each other. "Now, let's get this party started!" Emily cheered.

The End

Join Emily, Grace and Layla
for another adventure in ...

Whale Song Wedding

"There once was a mermaid with long golden hair . . ." The song filled the café. It was normally filled with happy chatter, but today all the customers were listening to the group of fishermen singing in the corner. "She had a tail as blue as the ocean deep . . ."

Emily crept round the tables, trying not to make any noise as she put an omelette down in front of a lady, who smiled and nodded in thanks. Emily tiptoed back to the counter and turned to watch the singers too.

"And barnacles on her bum! Oh! Barnacles on her bum!" the fishermen bellowed. The accordion and guitar played a jaunty tune and everyone in the café laughed and cheered as the song finished and the fishermen bowed.

Emily's dad gave them a thumbs-up from the kitchen door. The Sunday Musical Brunch was his idea, and it was going well so far. Emily's parents were much happier since they'd moved here and opened The Mermaid Café, and Emily was too. She loved living near the sea, even if the seagulls perched on her bedroom windowsill and squawked noisily early in the morning. And she loved hanging out with her best friends, Grace and Layla. But Emily's tummy turned over as she thought about what was about to happen now.

Grace went up to one of the fisherman, her grandad, and took the guitar from him. She looked like a real musician as she sat tuning it, wearing a stripy top, jeans, and a red headscarf over her blonde hair. Layla was already on the makeshift stage, tapping the microphone like a professional and smoothing down the yellow skirt that matched the yellow ribbons in her long, dark-brown hair. Her two friends were ready, the only thing missing . . . was her. Emily gulped as Layla waved her over.

Nervously, Emily took off her apron and went to stand next to her friends.

"Hi everyone, this is a song we wrote," Layla announced.

Grace gave Emily a supportive grin as she started playing. Together, they all started to sing:

"The oceans are big and beautiful,
The seas are wide and strong,
But we have to keep them clean
And put right what we've got wrong.
Tell people to stop using plastic,

Say they can't dump it in the sea,
So that all the mermaids and fishes
Can live happy and healthy and free."

Emily peeked out at the crowd. Everyone was nodding and tapping their feet. Over by the counter Mum and Dad were recording the performance on their phones, looking proud.

The three friends belted out the final chorus:

"We can all be Sea Keepers,
And work to save our seas,
So join us in our mission,
Won't you save our oceans . . . please?"

Grace gave the guitar one last strum and Layla hit a high note. Everyone clapped. Emily just felt glad it was over! She hugged her best friends.

"That was brilliant!" Mum said, smiling as Emily went over to the counter.

"Blueberry pancakes and orange juice?" Dad asked. Now that the singing was over and her nerves had settled down, Emily was suddenly very hungry!

Dad piled pancakes on a plate, and Emily went to share them with her friends. Grace was sitting with her mum, grandad and little brother Henry, and even her dog Barkley was lying under the table, happily eating a doggy treat. At the next table were Layla's parents and her big sister, Nadia. As Layla sat down,

Nadia went onstage and started singing a pop song.

"That was great, I want to be a Sea Keeper!" Grace's little brother said as Emily arrived.

Emily glanced at her friends over Henry's head, and they all shared a grin. No one knew what it *really* meant to be a Sea Keeper!

Emily, Grace and Layla had been magically chosen to become Sea Keepers when they'd met a mermaid princess and gone with her to the underwater city of Atlantis. There, the mermaids had told them about the evil siren, Effluvia, who was trying to take over the mermaid kingdom. Effluvia was trying to find the Golden Pearls that were filled with ancient mermaid magic. It was the Sea Keepers' job to find them first and use their magic for good instead of evil.

Nadia finished her song, and everyone clapped politely. But as she applauded, Emily saw something shimmer on her wrist – her bracelet was glowing. It was time for another Sea Keeper adventure! She quickly pulled her sleeve down over her bracelet. "Um, do you want to come up to my room?" she asked Grace and Layla. "I've got, er, something to show you?"

Grace nodded straight away, but Layla

was looking at the stage. "Hang on, Mr Singh from school is about to sing," she told them.

Emily elbowed her and showed her the bracelet. Layla gave an excited squeal as she realised what was going on.

"We're just going upstairs, it'll only take a second," Grace said to her family. She wasn't lying, because no time ever passed while they were off on an adventure. They could help the mermaids and still be back in time to listen to the teacher's song!

They rushed up the narrow stairs to Emily's bedroom in the flat above the cafe. Her big ginger cat, Nemo, was curled up on her bed as usual, and she could see the sea through her window. It looked so vast, it was hard to believe that in a few seconds they'd be out there somewhere, swimming with mermaids . . .

Read **Whale Song Wedding**
to find out what happens next!

How to be a real-life

Would you like to be a Sea Keeper just like Emily, Grace and Layla? Here are a few ideas for how you can help protect our oceans.

1. Try to use less water
Using too much water is wasteful. Turn off the tap when you brush your teeth and take shorter showers.

2. Use fewer plastic products
Plastic ends up in the ocean and can cause problems for marine wildlife. Instead of using plastic bottles, refill a metal bottle. Carry a tote bag when out shopping, and use non-disposable food containers and cutlery.

Sea Keeper

3. Help at a beach clean-up
Keeping the shore clear of litter
means less litter is swept into the sea.
Next time you're at the beach or a
lake, try and pick up all the litter
you can see.

4. Reduce your energy consumption
Turn off lights when you aren't using
a room. Walk or cycle instead of
driving. Take the stairs instead of the
lift. Using less energy helps reduce
the effects of climate change.

5. Avoid products that harm marine life
Do not buy items made from endangered species.
If you eat seafood, make sure it comes from
sustainable sources.

SEA KEEPERS

Dive into a mermaid adventure!

The Mermaid's Dolphin
Coral Ripley

The Sea Unicorn
Coral Ripley

Coral Reef Rescue
Coral Ripley

Sea Turtle School
Coral Ripley

Penguin Island
Coral Ripley

Sea Otter Summer Camp
Coral Ripley

The Rainbow Seahorse
Coral Ripley

Coming Soon

Whale Song Wedding
Coral Ripley

The Missing Manatee
Coral Ripley

Starfish Sleepover
Coral Ripley

Seal Cub Surprise
Coral Ripley